FUN FOR CHRIS

FUN FOR CHRIS

By BLOSSOM E. RANDALL

Pictures by

EUNICE YOUNG SMITH

ALBERT WHITMAN & COMPANY CHICAGO

To

AMY

New Printing 1969

© 1956, by ALBERT WHITMAN & COMPANY
L. C. Card No. 56–7753. Published simultaneously
in the Dominion of Canada by George J. McLeod,
Limited, Toronto. Lithographed in the U.S.A.

FOREWORD

It is extremely difficult to explain varia-
tions in skin color to young children who
are usually unaware of these differences
until they are pointed out to them.

Parents and teachers are constantly faced
with this problem and often ask for books
which they can use in order to help children
understand and accept all kinds of people.

Chris' mother answers his first questions
with honest simplicity.

Young children will enjoy this warm happy
story and adults will find Mrs. Randall's
approach a refreshing and helpful one.

Charlemae Rollins
Children's Librarian
Hall Branch, Chicago Public Library

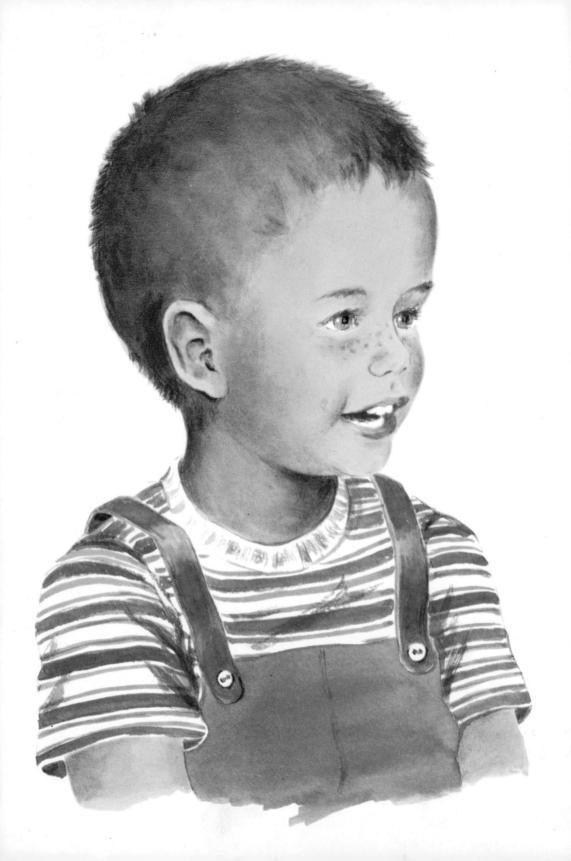

FUN FOR CHRIS

His real name was Christopher Allan, but his mother usually said just "Chris."

So, she would always say, "Chris, it's time to go to the store for groceries," or, "Chris, it's time to get ready for church," or, "Chris, it's time to pick up your toys."

But she always said, "Christopher
Allan, I love you!" when she tucked
him into his little bed at night.

Everyone loved Chris, for he knew how to show others how much he loved them.

He could put his arms around his grandmother's neck as quick as a wink when she came to see him.

Whenever someone did something nice just for him, he could say, "Thank you" so fast.

He even thanked the wind one day for opening the door for him when he ran out.

But anyone who looked at Chris knew he was a happy little boy. He had such a happy little face and was always ready to smile. There were six or seven freckles across his turned-up nose.

Chris had a nice back yard with a fence around it. He would play in it every day.

He had a big sandpile to dig in, and a swing to go high in, and a ladder to do tricks on.

But it was so much more fun when someone else, about his same size, could do all these things with him.

He had Roger and Sally and Steve in his family. But they were all bigger than he was. And most of the time, they were at school.

He had little Kathy, too. But she could only sit in her baby jumping-seat and laugh at him, or pat-a-cake for him.

He really needed someone else.

One day Chris was out playing in the sandpile with his rubber cowboys and Indians. He heard a funny squeak-squeak-squeak sound coming down the street.

He ran over to the fence to see what could be making the noise.

There he saw a little boy, pulling a
small red wagon behind him. The
wheels going round and round were
making that squeaky noise.

When Chris smiled and waved at the boy, he waved back at Chris and smiled.

When he smiled, his teeth looked so pretty and white. For the rest of him was so very brown—brown curly hair, brown sparkling eyes, brown face, brown hands, brown arms, and brown legs.

Chris then said, "Hi! I'm Chris. Who are you?"

The little boy laughed and answered, "I'm Toby."

"Can you stop and play with me?" asked Chris.

"I'm going to the store for my mother now," said Toby. "But maybe I can stop and play with you some time. I'll ask my mother."

Chris walked slowly back to the sandpile to play all alone again.

He wished that Toby would stop and play right then, because whenever Mother said "some time," it always seemed to be a long, long time away.

The very next morning, Chris came out of his house with his cars and trucks to put them in the sandpile.

There was Toby sitting near the gate, waiting for him.

Chris ran to get
Mother to open the
gate for him.

It was too hard for
Chris to open.

Then he said, "Mother, this is Toby,
and he came to play with me."

"Hello, Toby," said Mother, "how long can you stay to play?"

"Not very long," answered Toby, "because I promised to get some bread for my mother."

"Have fun!" called Mother as she went back into the house.

She wished that she could stay outdoors with Chris and Toby and just have fun, too. But she had to wash the dishes and sweep the floor and iron some clothes. Toby and Chris did have fun together. Mother could hear them laughing and talking all the time she was working in the house.

Toby was a little older than Chris, and he could show Chris how to do some things he had never done before.

180549 15

The nicest thing he taught Chris
that first day was how to make a long
tunnel in the sand.

First, he piled the sand away up
high in a great tall mountain. Then
he began digging with his hand from
one side, and Chris began digging with
his hand from the other side.

Before long, they were touching each other's fingers.

They had reached the middle and their long tunnel was finished. Chris would push his little trucks and cars from one side of his mountain right through to the other side. Then Toby would pull them out.

As they played in the sand together, Chris put his arm close to Toby's arm and said, "See how brown your arm looks when it's next to mine."

Toby then put his bare foot next to Chris' foot, wiggled his short toes, and said, "My foot is a lot browner than your foot, too."

At this, Chris asked, "Toby, are you brown all up and down, or just on the part of you that I can see outside your clothes?"

"I'm all brown," answered Toby "See?" He pulled up his yellow T-shirt so that Chris could see his brown stomach.

Chris leaned over and patted it, and it felt smooth and warm, just like his own stomach.

When Toby had to go, Chris said, "Be sure to come back again to play."

And Toby did, almost every day.

And when Mother would kiss Chris goodnight and say, "Christopher Allan, I love you," Chris would answer, "I love you, Mother, and I love Toby, too."

One Saturday, when Toby and Chris were doing monkey tricks on the ladder, another little boy named Jimmy came over to the gate.

Jimmy lived not very far away. He was older than Chris and Toby, so he was at school every day but Saturday and Sunday.

"Come on in, Jimmy," called Chris from high up on the ladder.

"Why are you playing with that black boy?" asked Jimmy.

"He's my friend Toby," answered Chris. "And he's not really black. He's brown, and he's lots of fun to play with."

Toby hurried down the ladder. "Good-bye, Chris. I have to go now," he said.

But Chris cried, "Don't go, Toby.

"Mother! Mother! Toby is going to leave me!"

He pushed himself through the rungs of the ladder and dropped to the ground. Then he ran to Toby and took him by the hand.

Mother came running out of the house.

"What's the matter, boys?" she asked, as she put an arm around Chris and an arm around Toby.

Then Chris asked, "Mother, why *is* Toby all brown?"

"Because," said Mother, "that is the way God planned him to be.

"Toby's mother and father have nice brown skin, so he is like them. Daddy and I are lighter than his mother and father, so you are like us.

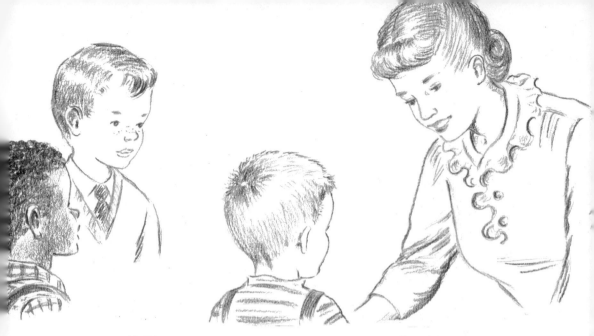

"Jimmy's mother and father are lighter than Toby's mother and father, too.

"I'll tell you boys something. Let's pretend all the children in this big world were playing in this back yard.

"You would all see many more children here with dark skin than with light skin like yours and Jimmy's."

"I didn't know that," said Chris.

"But you did know they would all like to swing in your swing and play in your sandpile?" Mother asked.

"Yes," laughed Chris. "I knew that. All of us like to play!"

Then Toby asked, "Why would there be more children with dark skin?"

Mother replied, "Because there are more mothers and fathers with dark skin.

"Children always look like their mothers and fathers in some way."

"Is that why people are always saying I have my daddy's red hair?" asked Jimmy.

"Yes, Jimmy," said Mother. "Your red hair is the way you are like your daddy.

"Chris has dimples just like mine; and Toby has brown skin and curly hair just like his mother and daddy.

"If you'll watch, you'll see that we are all like our mothers and fathers.

"You can understand that everything happens just the way God plans it to happen.

"And we grow up with the ones who know best how to love us and take care of us."

As Mother finished, she gave a big hug to Chris and a big hug to Toby.

Then Chris led Toby over to Jimmy.
He smiled at Jimmy and said, "I
play with Toby almost every day
because he's my very best friend. Come
on in our yard and have fun with us!"
And that's just what Jimmy did.

Wisconsin State College at Eau Claire
LIBRARY RULES

———

No book should be taken from the library until it has been properly charged by the librarian.

Books may be kept two weeks and may be renewed for a one week period.

A fine of ten cents a day will be charged for books kept over time.

In case of loss or injury the person borrowing this book will be held responsible for the value of a new book, plus processing.

Due	DUE	Due	DUE
JL 8 '70			
JL 15 '70			
OCT 9 '70			
NOV 25 '70			
DEC 4 '70			
NO 24 '70			
JA 15 '71			
FE 2 '71			
MR 4 '71			
JUN 25 '71			
OC 27 '71			
NOV 4 '71			
NOV 1 0 1971			
NOV 6 '72			
NOV 14 '72			